MR.UPPITY

by Roger Hargreaves

EGMONT WORLD LIMITED.

This is the story of Mr Uppity and how Mr Uppity finishes this story not quite so uppity as at the beginning of the story.

You see, Mr Uppity was one of the rudest people in the world, if not the rudest.

He was rude to anybody and everybody. So of course in Bigtown, which was where he lived, he had no friends at all.

Not one!

"Miserable old Uppity," they used to call him, and he certainly looked it!

Now as well as being rude, Mr Uppity was also rich. Very rich! One of the richest people in the world, if not the richest.

He had the largest, longest limousine in Bigtown.

He had the largest, longest garden in Bigtown.

He had, on top of the hill in the middle of Bigtown, the most enormous house. The biggest house in Bigtown.

And there he lived.

All alone.

Miserable old Uppity.

One day, Mr Uppity was walking in the gardens of his enormous house when suddenly he heard a voice. A little voice.

"Hello," said the voice.

Mr Uppity looked, and there, in one of his hundreds of flower beds, was a goblin.

"Aren't you going to say hello to me?" asked the goblin.

"Go away!" said Mr Uppity, rudely.

"Oh, I know who you must be," said the goblin. "You must be Mr Uppity who's rude to everybody!"

"Hmph!" sniffed Mr Uppity, rudely.

"Well I know somebody who wants to meet you," said the goblin, and skipped off, the way goblins do.

"Come on," he called over his shoulder.

Mr Uppity's curiosity got the better of him.

He followed.

"In there," said the goblin, pointing at a small hole in a tree.

"Don't be silly," snorted Mr Uppity.

"Oh, I'm not being silly," said the goblin.

"Yes you are," snapped Mr Uppity. "I can't possibly get in there!"

"Aha," smiled the goblin, and then he said a magic word known only to goblins, which sounded like "Wobblygobblygook!" or something like that.

Suddenly, Mr Uppity started shrinking. He shrank and he shrank until he was exactly the same size as the goblin.

"Turn me back to my proper size at once," spluttered Mr Uppity in a rage.

"Shan't!" grinned the goblin.

And so saying the goblin climbed through the hole into the tree.

Poor Mr Uppity didn't know what to do, so he followed him.

Inside the tree there was a staircase going down, and down.

Do you know where it led to?

It led directly to the Kingdom of the Goblins!

That's where!

"I demand to be taken IMMEDIATELY to whoever is in charge," said Mr Uppity, angrily.

"Oh you shall, you shall," grinned the goblin.

And he led Mr Uppity through the streets of the Kingdom of the Goblins until they came to a palace.

"Halt! Who goes there?" cried the goblin sentry at the gate.

"I have brought Mr Uppity," said the goblin.

"Oh," said the sentry, and smiled.

The goblin and Mr Uppity passed through the gates and into a courtyard and through some more gates and along a long corridor and through some large gold doors and into a huge room.

There, sitting on a gold throne, was the King of the Goblins.

"Your Majesty," announced the goblin, bowing low. "May I present Mr Uppity."

"Ah," said the King. "So you're the fellow who goes about being rude to everybody and doesn't have any friends!"

"Nonsense!" said Mr Uppity, rudely.

"I can see that what I've heard is true," said the King looking at the indignant Mr Uppity. "You're much too puffed up with your own importance!"

"Therefore," he continued, "I am going to allow you to be turned back to your proper size. But when you get back to Bigtown, if you're rude to anybody, anybody at all, you will immediately shrink to the size you are now. Do you understand?"

The goblin then took Mr Uppity back through the Kingdom of the Goblins, and up the staircase, and out of the tree at the bottom of Mr Uppity's gardens.

The goblin looked at Mr Uppity and said something which sounded like "Koogylbogylbbow!" or something, which is probably "Wobblygobblygook!" said backwards, and Mr Uppity grew and grew back to his original size.

"Now you remember what the King said," warned the goblin. "Don't be so uppity in future!"

Mr Uppity marched off furiously up to his enormous house.

The following day Mr Uppity was out walking through the streets of Bigtown.

Suddenly, he came across a little boy playing with a ball.

"Get out of my way!" snapped Mr Uppity, rudely.

But, as soon as he'd said it, you know what happened, don't you?

Yes!

Mr Uppity shrank and shrank until he was no bigger than the ball the boy was playing with.

"Oh dear," he gasped, and then he thought.

"I'm sorry," he said to the boy. "What I meant to say was, 'Please could I get past?'"

Immediately Mr Uppity grew to his original size, and the boy moved, and Mr Uppity went on his way.

Then he met an old lady carrying a large shopping basket.

She was late for market.

"Excuse me," she said to Mr Uppity. "Could you tell me the time, please?"

"No!" said Mr Uppity, rudely.

But, as soon as he'd said it, you know what happened, don't you?

Yes!

Mr Uppity shrank and shrank until he could easily have fitted into the old lady's basket.

"Oh dear," he gasped, and then he thought.

"I'm sorry," he said to the old lady. "What I meant to say was, 'It's twenty-five past eleven!'"

Immediately Mr Uppity grew to his original size, and the old lady thanked him, and Mr Uppity went on his way.

Then he went and bought a newspaper from a man standing on the corner of the main street in Bigtown.

He was just about to walk away, when suddenly he stopped and thought.

He turned back to the man and said, "Thank you!"

'Thank you' were two words Mr Uppity had never used before.

The man smiled.

A smile was something Mr Uppity wasn't used to getting.

Then Mr Uppity was stopped by a man who asked him if he could tell him the way to the bank.

Mr Uppity was about to say "No!" when he thought.

"Yes!" he said, and told the man.

"Thank you!" said the man.

'Thank you' were words Mr Uppity not only had never used before but were words he had never had said to him before.

Mr Uppity smiled. He felt happy.

Happy was a feeling Mr Uppity wasn't used to feeling.

He liked it!

And do you know, from that day forward to this day backward, Mr Uppity is a changed person.

He's still the richest person in Bigtown, perhaps the richest person in the world, but now he has lots of friends.

And he smiles a lot.

And he never gets that shrinking feeling.

And do you know which words Mr Uppity uses most of all these days?

'Please' and 'Thank you'.

So, what we'd like to say is, 'Thank you' for reading this story.

And, if you're ever thinking about being rude to somebody, 'Please' keep a sharp lookout for goblins!